drawing lessons

TRACY MACK

scholastic press
NEW YORK

I would like to thank my wonderful writer's group—Anne Burt, Stephanie Morecraft, Ann Somerhausen, and Andrea Sheridan—whose insight, sensitivity, and unflagging dedication have contributed greatly to this story.

Very special thanks also to Billy Goda, my friend and mentor, for sharing so much wisdom about writing and life.

To Anne Dunn, whose editorial vision, guidance, and passion are truly a work of art.

To Marijka Kostiw, design goddess, who always inspires me.

And especially to Michael Citrin, who fills my every day with color and light.

ISBN 0-439-11202-8

LIBRARY OF CONGRESS CATALOG CARD NUMBER: 99-27254

10 9 8 7 6 5 4 3 2 1   0/0 01 02 03 04 05

Printed in the U.S.A.   23
First edition, March 2000

Text type was set in Cochin 12/18.
Display type was set in Lady Dawn TR.

Book design by Marijka Kostiw

for my mother and father,
my deep, strong roots

And she shall be like a tree
planted by the rivers of water
that bringeth forth her fruit in her season. . . .

—psalm 1

I realized that I had things in my head
not like what I had been taught —
not like what I had seen —

    shapes and ideas so familiar to me
that it hadn't occurred to me to put them down.
I decided to stop painting,
to put away everything that I had done,
and to start to say the things that were my own.

—georgia o'keeffe

crack!

Dad's chain saw cut a thick branch. It snapped dead at the joint and landed with a thunk at the base of the tree. I was on the back porch steps with Nicky, watching, and trying to draw the tall oak in my sketchbook before it was too late.

The saw whined as it spiraled through branch after branch, slicing until there was nothing left but a single stalk of tree pressed up against the late-afternoon indigo sky. One minute the branches were reaching to me from the wide trunk like outstretched arms. Then they were gone.

"Does he have to do it?" Nicky said into the air. My best friend's elbows perched on her knees and her hands covered her ears to block the noise. The two of us had been coming to this tree forever. It was where we held our secret meetings when we had the spy club that was made up of just Nicky and me. We were too old for that now, but still, it was hard to say good-bye.

This was where we swung from the long braided rope that Dad had hung from a high branch, bringing kids from all over the neighborhood. Once Nicky let herself fall on purpose, hoping to break an arm and get a cast like her brother Jonah's, all colored in with his friends' names in bright markers. In the end, she only sprained her thumb and had to wear an ugly metal splint that no one could sign. She got mad when I laughed and didn't call me for three whole days. But we could joke about that now.

It was this tree that taught me about looking,

really looking. I remember that first April when I began to see. It had been raining for two weeks straight, but on that day it was sunny and warm and the air coming through the screen in my bedroom smelled sugary and wet. I'd had the chicken pox and wasn't allowed to leave the house at all, not even to walk with Dad and our dog, Cassidy, down the driveway to get the mail. This was the first day I was really better.

"Daddy," I had yelled. "Daddy, please can I go outside? Please, please, please! The trees are leaving."

He walked into my room, rubbing a paintbrush clean with an old cloth rag. "Where are they going?" he asked.

"They're not *going* anywhere. They're just leaving," I said, pointing out the window. "Can't we go and see?"

"Sure," he said, looking puzzled. "We'd better go and say good-bye. Do you think we should pack them some lunch?" he asked, thinking this was some game I was playing. "Who knows how long they'll be gone."

"Daddy!" I squealed. I was still in my night-gown, but I grabbed his hand and pulled him along behind me into the bright, warm day.

"See," I said, pointing to the big oak.

Bright yellow-green baby leaves poked out of the thin, spare limbs, brilliant with color and laughing in the sunshine.

Dad's mouth dropped open. "Wow, Rory, you weren't kidding."

We both stood there then, quiet and still, looking at the tree and at the golden morning light that lit its leaves from the underside and made them glow.

I never imagined the leaving time would mean anything else.

There was a snap of cool wind, carrying the scent of sawdust and a sweetness off the river. It was the last day of summer vacation, and already the leaves had begun to turn, their edges brighter than ever before. Shiny yellows, burnt oranges, golden reds. I kept sketching as if the branches were still there, filling them in from memory.

Dad was back on the ground now, jimmying the saw blade. Its giant silver teeth glinted like a mouth full of braces.

"You guys okay?" Mom opened the kitchen door to let Cassidy out, and he came straight to me.

"No!" Nicky didn't take her eyes off the tree. It looked naked and frail.

Mom stepped out onto the porch, put her hand on my head, and peered over my shoulder at the sketch. "Get it all down," she said and then stared off at the gnarled pile of branches.

I looked at the gray wool socks poking through her chunky sandals. Her voice was calm, but in my head, she was still pleading with my father.

"Couldn't we try to treat it, Peter?"

He'd just stared at her. "It's already dead."

You'd never know there was anything wrong

with the tree. It didn't *look* sick. But it had some disease you couldn't see, and that's what made it so dangerous. Even though its branches were sturdy, its leaves thick and full, and it watched over our yard like a healthy, normal tree, it was dying on the inside. If a big storm came, it might knock it right over onto the house. It would fall straight through the skylight into my bedroom.

None of us wanted to do it, but we had to cut the tree down. That's why I was sketching the tree and why getting the sketch right was so important. I'd never made a finished drawing of the tree before. I knew it so well I had never thought to record it. But now, I wouldn't have the tree if I forgot any part of it — its proud posture or its palm-shaped leaves with their delicate fingers — and I'd need it for the mural that Dad had agreed to help me paint as a surprise for Mom's birthday. It might make up a little for the gaping hole in our yard, and maybe, if the mural was very, very good, and if she could see that Dad had worked hard on it, too, it could heal the yellow hurt that melted through her eyes more and more lately. Yellow is the saddest color I know.

Dad picked up the saw and steadied himself. He flipped the switch. The wail of the engine cut the air like a siren. Cassidy let out a yelp and nudged his head under my leg.

"It's okay, boy." I patted his ear.

The saw vibrated in Dad's arms and his whole body shook under the weight of it.

I stared at the thick trunk, its bark old and weathered. In my mind's eye, I saw Dad perched on a low branch, dressed in a black unitard, painted into a skeleton one Halloween. He had his guitar strapped across him and was singing "Dry Bones" at the top of his voice. And Cassidy was sitting by the trunk, howling out some kind of miserable harmony. Mom and I had nearly fallen down laughing at the sight of them.

The saw made a low, steady trill now as it neared the center of the tree. Soon the cut would be more than halfway, and the tree wouldn't have the strength to hold itself up. I felt like screaming, "Don't! Please." But it was no use.

The tree was bending now, like an old man stooped over a cane. My hand froze on the paper. The tree fell slowly, bones cracking from the inside. Then, before it hit the ground, it seemed to sway just the tiniest bit toward me, away from the woods Dad was aiming for.

Good-bye, tree.

a week later, I sat on the fat stump. Its surface was still rough from the saw, and a rotted-out hole gutted the center. I penciled in a few more shadows on my drawing while Nicky lay reading on the grass beside me. Her head rested on Cassidy's belly. What was taking Dad so long?

I reached into my knapsack for an eraser and rubbed it gently into the paper the way he had taught me, to get the modeled effect. Already my knapsack was stuffed with books. Secretly, I was happy that summer had melted away. Not happy about being a seventh grader at Hillview Middle School so much as the coming of autumn, my favorite season. Something about the way the trees produced the richest palette and the air turned suddenly sharp and soft at the same time and the river rose up and showed its strength.

Now that we had moved to the upper wing with the eighth graders, things felt different. The hallways were jammed with kids much taller than me, and the bathrooms smelled smoky and sour. But there were good things, too. Our lockers were bigger. And we had free study periods because, as my English teacher, Ms. Meadow, had put it, we weren't babies anymore. "This is junior high," she'd said on the first day. "No more coddling." I don't know why, but that felt good and scary at the same time, like when I introduced a new element into a drawing and it took a while to figure out if it was working.

Nicky was more excited about school than I was. And it wasn't just that she was smarter. Nicky could talk to anyone and she was never shy about speaking up in class, even when she wasn't sure of the answer, which was almost never. I wished I could be more like that. Nicky's mom said that opposites attract and that Nicky and I complemented each other. I could see it. If Nicky was a lively, bright red, I was a steady, quiet green.

"We'll probably have boyfriends this year," Nicky had predicted over the summer. But we had known the boys in our class since kindergarten, and I couldn't picture any of them as my boyfriend. Besides, no guy had ever looked at me like he was considering me as a girlfriend. I was thin and small, three inches shorter than Nicky when we last measured against her closet door. I wouldn't mind if it was always just the two of us, laughing at things no one else could understand, inventing new languages only we could speak. My mom and her best friend, Carol, were that way — so tight it was almost as if they were sisters.

It was Nicky who named our languages,

because she was better with words. There was Hotsy Totsy, where every word began with the letter T, and Fish, where everything ended in SH, and Dog Latin, in honor of Cassidy. But we didn't tell anyone how that went.

Mom called Nicky a linguist. She was taking French and Latin this year, and she and her brothers already spoke fluent Spanish. Mrs. Abrams was from Argentina and talked to the kids only in Spanish when they were babies. Nicky wanted to be a translator for the U.N. when she grew up.

Nicky brushed dried leaves from her sweater and rolled over to kiss Cassidy on the nose. He lapped his big tongue across her whole mouth and she laughed. "I have to go look at invitations with my mom. You know how nuts she gets over this New Year's Eve party every year. I swear, it's only September."

She pulled on her Rollerblades and clicked the toggles shut. "You coming?"

"I have to talk to my dad," I said, working the gummy eraser around the base of my tree.

"Call me later," and she clomped across the lawn.

Cassidy lifted his head and then fell back on the grass with a short moan. I studied my drawing for a minute.

"Dad . . . ?" I called into the barn where he was painting.

"Not now, Ror."

I looked at my watch. It was already 4:30. If Mom left the office on time, she could be home in a couple of hours.

I got up and walked to the barn door, opened it a crack. "How much longer?"

"About an hour." He was standing at his easel, looking at his model and sliding a piece of charcoal across the canvas. "Okay, honey?"

"I just want to show you something. . . ."

Dad looked up, distracted. "Can it wait a little?"

The woman looked over, too, without breaking   13

her pose, and smiled. A piece of cream-colored cloth was draped in gentle folds over her bare body, and she was stretched out across a small wooden platform.

"I'm going to the river, then." I cradled the sketchbook behind my back and forced a smile.

I needed him to tell me if my tree was finished.

i clipped Cassidy's leash onto his bright purple collar. He was eager for a good run. Then I emptied the books from my knapsack, put in my sketchbook, pencils, and eraser, and pulled the straps over both my shoulders.

The air felt good on my cheeks, lifted up my hair, and tossed it behind me as we flew down the windy hills, past the enormous stone houses that made our smaller wooden one look like "the carriage house to somebody's mansion," according to Mom. But I disagreed. Our house was cozy and familiar. I loved how we could hear each other from every room. How would we fill all the rooms in one of those big places anyway? Wouldn't it feel weird to have furniture that never got sat on sprawling about in every direction?

Cassidy and I crossed the bridge over the train tracks and climbed down to our favorite flat rock at the edge of the water. The hills across the Hudson River rippled with color, tumbling down to the water in waves of plum and gold. The horizon fell in smoky layers to a line of tangerine sky that rested on the treetops. I could see an ocean filled with distant lands. I could see the end of the earth as it curved down to nowhere.

One day in Nicky's room, we wrote down all the places we were going to travel to when we got older.

"Rome!" I declared, picturing myself inside the Sistine Chapel, gazing up at Michelangelo's ceiling until my neck ached.

"And Russia," Nicky added. "And we have to go to Spain because my cousin Emily studied there and she said Spanish guys are the hottest."

I just rolled my eyes.

Paris was on our list, too, of course. I was dying to go to the Louvre Museum and see the Venus di Milo and the Mona Lisa and the giant Rubens nudes. My dad says you could spend your whole life in there and still not see everything.

Water slapped at the rocks, sometimes wetting my sneakers, and Cassidy tried to catch the spray in his mouth. They should call this the River Hudson, I thought as I slipped the loop of his leash around my ankle. The river should come first.

I pulled out my sketchbook, a Pentalic HB pencil — the kind Dad liked — and turned to the picture of our tree. It seemed to need a little more work. "Preliminary sketches are important. . . ." His voice was clear in my head. "They guide you, the way an outline helps you write an essay." When

I'd finally get it right, he'd look at me and nod. "That's it." And a warm feeling would spread out inside me like drinking hot chocolate on a cold day.

I looked up at the feathery clouds, the rosy sky on the cusp of sunset.

"If I worked at home, I'd never miss the pink sunsets," Mom had said a few weeks ago.

And I saw Dad's jaw clench.

It was Mom's job at the publishing house that paid for everything — groceries, bills, school supplies, clothes. I wished she didn't have to work late all the time.

"We can't afford not knowing where the next mortgage payment is coming from. And we need the insurance," she'd say and let out a long, tired sigh. Then Dad would shut the kitchen door too hard and head for his studio.

But if Mom had a beautiful mural painted on our barn wall and she could go in there and have her pink sunsets anytime, early in the morning or even late at night, maybe that would help. Maybe it would remind her of our arts-and-crafts Saturdays when we'd all press wildflowers or mix homemade paper for stationery or capture butterflies long enough to study the color and pattern of their wings before letting them fly free. Art connected all of us then. But that seemed like so long ago. Maybe the mural would help me remember, too.

My pencil shimmied across the page, soft lead whispering to paper. That's what I'd told Dad when we first started the drawing lessons: "The pencil tells the paper what to make."

A smile wiggled out the side of his mouth. "I think you will be a true artist," he'd said.

I was five then. And every Sunday we'd sit in his big barn studio, side by side at the drawing table, with huge pieces of paper stretched out in front of us. "We don't want to limit ourselves," he would say. It was always late in the afternoon, and the last bits of pink sun fell in through a corner of the window onto the small still life of fruit he had arranged.

"Pay attention to the light, Rory," he would tell me. "Don't sketch the banana as you know a banana looks. Watch the light and draw what you see." He would tilt his head and move his pencil across the paper as he continued. "Look at the object. See how it sits in the space? Notice the way the light hits it." Sometimes he would pull me onto his lap and wrap his big hand around mine to show me, the soft sunlight warming my hand in his, protective and steady.

A whole shelf in my closet was lined with sketchbooks. I liked to look back at the old ones from when I was just a little kid. Mostly they were filled with pictures of my family — Mom with lots of hair and her arms coming out of her head, Cassidy with three legs and a giant tail, Dad with two big, round eyes and no mouth.

The later sketchbooks were from the drawing

lessons with Dad — there was one that was all still lifes and some of the human figure, and others of landscapes where I was learning how to create perspective. Now that I was older, I could draw from my head, without concentrating so much on the object. But Dad said it was important to know the basics first.

I didn't have lessons very often anymore. Dad said, more than instruction, I needed practice.

When I looked back over all the books, I could see how much progress I'd made. I could also see my father and how much my drawings looked like his. "Look at the light, Rory," the comforting voice in my head reminded me. "Watch how it moves."

I have never told anyone that for as long as I can remember, before Dad's paintings helped pay for things and then didn't, and even before the drawing lessons, I have thought in colors. Blue for a gentle song, for Dad's painting of me as a baby, hanging above the dresser in their bedroom — the one he titled "Rory's Lullaby," where I am nuzzled in Mom's arms beneath a cloudless evening sky. Pink for laughter, for the giggling water lilies at the museum in New York City that my parents first took me to see when I was three, and I sat on the floor of that big room and laughed out loud and would not move. Silver for imagination, for the glistening rings that circled and swelled inside my head when I squeezed my eyes shut very tight, just before the pictures formed.

I saw pictures in everything, in the shadows the clouds drew, in the sounds painted on the wind. So when the drawing lessons began and my father showed me to watch the way light changes shapes and colors, molting and massaging them into surprising forms, it was like something shifting and settling into place inside me. It was like I already knew, the way Nicky says a new language slips off your tongue unexpectedly when it becomes your own.

The light pressed stronger through the clouds

now, turning rose to amber, and I saw the mural painted across my mind.

I told Dad that he and I should each bring something of our own to the painting. It didn't have to be true to the picture we really saw from our backyard. We could add whatever we wanted to make it unique. Then we would watch the mural unfold very slowly.

"That's the great thing about painting," Dad said. "You can create your own imaginary world to live in."

I shut my eyes and looked at the river landscape laid out inside them. I would paint our tree, standing strong and tall, on the bank of the river.

That was the great thing about painting, I thought. *You could bring back something you'd lost and keep it forever.*

dad was washing dirty pots when I got home. His hair was pulled into a low ponytail, but one short piece kept falling in front of his eyes. There were suds on his forehead from where he had tried to push it away.

"Dad," I whispered, even though I knew Mom wasn't home yet. "When can we start?"

He turned to look at me. The slightest shadow moved across his eyes. He was inside one of his paintings, in some faraway world. "Tomorrow?"

"I'm supposed to go to a track meet with Nicky."

Dad nodded.

"Thursday's good," I said.

"Yeah," he said softly into the sink. "As soon as possible."

He wasn't paying attention anymore. He didn't even hear me ask if I should dry the pots. Dad seemed to disappear into himself more and more lately.

Where does he go when he goes away like that?

I shifted the knapsack on my shoulder and felt the press of my sketchbook. Maybe now wasn't the time to show him.

I hung Cassidy's leash on the hook by the door and took the stairs two at a time to my room. It could wait until tomorrow. I pictured myself opening the book on the drawing table in front of him, the slow tilt of his head, the quiet nod, and finally, after a long pause, "Yes, that's it."

"*this place* looks cool. O-A-X-A-C-A," Nicky said the next day after school as she flipped through *Travel and Leisure* magazine. "How do you say that?" She curved her mouth into various fish poses. "Oh-ax-a-ca. Oxe-a-ca."

"Where is it?" I pulled the Jewel CD from its case and slid it into the player.

"Mexico."

In the basement beneath Nicky's room, her oldest brother Sam started slamming at his drums. One loud bang made Jewel's voice shake and jump.

"Aargh. Turn it up, Rory."

I hit the remote quickly, before she could yell through the vent for him to stop. I plopped down on the bed beside Nicky and started playing with her long, wavy hair. "You already speak Spanish."

"Yeah, but it says here there are many thriving Indian languages spoken there. I could record some of them." She turned the page and continued reading. "Hey, Ror, listen to this. 'Known for its weavers and artisans, Oxe-a-ca' — "

"Wa-HA-ca." Nicky's brother Jonah stood in the doorway. "It's pronounced Wa-HA-ca."

"Thanks." She tossed the word over her shoulder.

"No sweat. What's up, Michelangelo?" Jonah waved an arm before disappearing from the doorway. He was two years older than us. He had these amazing hazel eyes, and there was something so warm and steady about him, something a lot like Cassidy. Nicky and I joked that maybe Jonah was a dog in a past life.

"'Wa-HA-ca is an ancient city with a long artistic tradition,'" Nicky continued. "'Today, it is home to a new generation of painters whose work reflects the provocative melding of modern political concerns with the textures of their rich cultural heritage.' It's perfect for us."

Jewel's silvery voice fell out of the speakers and wound its way around the room, past the Audrey Hepburn posters — one from *Sabrina* and the other from *Roman Holiday* — that hung on the closet doors. Above the bed was a painting of Nicky and me on the rope swing that Dad had made when Nicky turned ten. "The dynamic duo hits the double digits" is what the card from our family had said.

I studied the lines and shadows on the painting. It always amazed me how Dad could get it just right, the curve of our mouths laughing, the twine of our fingers around the rope, and the perfect blending of colors.

Nicky tossed the magazine to the floor. "We should go. Dean's meet starts at 4:30."

Dean Barnes was a runner who Nicky had a huge crush on. He also happened to be my science partner. He had never said more to Nicky than "Your brother's a good athlete," but that was enough to make her hope that maybe he liked her, too.

"I can't," I told her, changing my mind about going. "My dad and I are getting the paint today."

"I don't want to sit in the bleachers by myself. He'll totally know." She looked hurt.

"I'm sorry, Nick, but we have to get started on the mural. We don't have a lot of time left."

There was something in Dad's voice last night that said we needed to begin right away. Deadlines freaked him out. When he had an exhibition, he always panicked and got kind of spaced out. He would disappear into his studio for days so he could be ready on time. Mom's birthday was only a couple of months away. That had to be why he was so distracted lately.

"We'll go to the next one, okay?" I said. Sometimes I wondered if Nicky was a little jealous that I spent so much time with my dad, because her father worked long hours for a big law firm in New York City. There were nights when she didn't even see him before she went to sleep.

Nicky pulled her lips to the side. "Yeah, all right."

I slid the elastic out of my own hair and wound it around the bottom of the French braid I'd made in hers before getting up to go. I stopped for a second in the doorway. "You can be the first to see it, you know. Even before we show my mom."

"I better be first, Rory Forrester!"

i dropped my knapsack by the tree stump and headed for the barn. I could hear faint laughter coming from inside. I knew Dad's session wasn't over yet, but I didn't care. I just had to show him the tree sketch and tell him we could start when he was done. I shut my eyes for a second and the mural came, like sunlight illuminating a patch of shade.

The door was half-open.

"Da —" I started to say, but the words stopped short in my throat.

"Oh, my God." The woman pulled the cloth up around her shoulders and leaned away from my father whose hand was cradling the back of her head, smoothing her long black hair. His lips were pressed against her ear.

I don't know if the next sound came from her or me, but she stuck a fist in her mouth as if to stop a scream.

Dad spun around, his eyes quick and sharp.

"Rory. What are you . . . ? I thought you and Nick . . ."

But I could barely hear him. I just stood there stiff, staring at her big, frightened eyes and his. A heat spread through my chest and burned down into my stomach.

He started to move toward me. "Rory, it's not what you think. . . ." He came closer and reached for me.

"Get away!" I screamed. "Don't touch me!"

Then I was running as fast as I could. My feet were moving across the grass and I didn't feel them.

It doesn't matter where they take me, I thought. And then all my thoughts scattered — like loose papers in the wind. The trees blurred and tilted into one another. But I kept going, propelled by a pounding inside that wouldn't let me stop.

I swatted branches from the path. My breath came in ragged pieces. A pain sliced down my chest. But I kept running.

The woods closed in around me, hard browns, flat greens. I tried to pull some air into my lungs, and it hurt. My legs were burning. But I pushed myself through the woods, through some strange picture in my mind. I was aiming straight for the vanishing point. I wanted more than anything to get there, to the end of the painting.

The hard dirt path snaked through the trees. Roots rose up, like giant feet, and tripped me until I went skidding onto the palms of my hands. Suddenly there was just the darkness and the prison of trunks.

I fell against a tree and let my back scrape down its tough bark. I picked a small pebble from my hand and started to cry. The colors dripped together in miserable, restless strokes, smearing the last clear images.

The sky didn't help. It broke the darkness with only a sigh of light, a milky, flat gray, stretched out above the trees like a dirty bedsheet.

A bird cried out from somewhere.

Suddenly, I felt scared in here. "It's dangerous," Mom had said. "You never know," Dad warned. Because bad kids hung out in these woods. Drinking, smoking. Doing things with girls . . .

I put myself back in the barn, watching his hand smooth her hair. I swallowed a dull ache in my throat. *How could you do that to Mom? How could you be such a jerk?*

The woman's dark, startled eyes glowed bright in my head. Did Mom know?

"It's not what you think, Rory."

What did that mean? That he wasn't really

kissing her? Maybe he was just repositioning her into a new pose. Was that possible? Could it be that this was all a big misunderstanding? Maybe he was waiting at the kitchen table now, wanting to explain.

A small sliver of light appeared, crested on the forest floor. It swelled ever so slightly and led me back to the foreground, back to the beginning, where his words were playing themselves over in my mind and gaining strength.

"It's not what you think, Rory."

"*hi, hon.*" Mom stood by the kitchen table and shook off her coat.

It was only 5:30. What was she doing home?

"Where've you been?" she asked, fitting the coat around the back of a chair and sitting down.

"At the river."

Dad was peeling carrots into the sink. He turned to me for a moment and shot me a look that said, I know that's not true because I was there.

I started picking at the scrape on my hand.

"I was just telling Dad what a dreadful day it

was. Three people were let go from their jobs . . ."

I was only half listening. I was trying to read Dad's mood. He couldn't have told her.

"I don't know how far back they think they can cut and still make books." She let out her breath and pulled her fingers through loose curls.

Suddenly I paid attention.

She reached out a hand to me as if she'd read my thoughts. "They haven't called my number yet." She looked over at my father, who had his back to us. "Don't worry, hon. You've still got your patron." She let out a sharp, sarcastic laugh.

A pain shot through my stomach, and I couldn't help but glare at her.

Dad was silent, but the rhythm of his strokes got faster.

"I'm going to take a shower." Mom stood up and kissed the top of my head as she passed.

I stayed by the kitchen table and waited for Dad to say something. He pushed the carrot peels into the drain opening and flipped the disposal switch.

Aren't you going to explain? Aren't you even going to look at me?

He switched off the disposal and turned around. Except for the soft pelts from the shower upstairs, it was quiet as a stone. His green eyes locked into mine.

Say something. Say anything.

He stood there looking at me, his face clenched tight, words pushing at the surface. His mouth opened and started to curve around a word.

I tried to reach to him through the silence.

He looked at me hard. The light behind his eyes seemed dim and blurred, like looking at a picture underwater.

Just say it, Dad, please explain.

"I'm going to walk Cassidy," he said and was gone.

an uneasy red shook inside me. A loud color, jumpy and impatient under my skin. Was he just going to pretend that nothing had happened?

I rifled through kitchen drawers and found what I needed. *Fine*, I thought, as I ran outside and dug the sketchbook out of my knapsack, still lying by the tree stump. *You'll never see my tree!*

One strike against a rock and the match blazed in my hand. I held it under the book. A single lick of flame and it caught, bringing the angry color alive. The black cover bubbled and crackled, giving off a sickening rubbery smell. The paper took next. Blue-orange tongues of fire tugged at one another. Bits of fine gray dust spiraled upward and made me cough.

There was nothing else, just the broken sky, like cracked plaster, and night coming on all at once, swallowing the day whole — taking the river sketches, the house and barn studies, taking the tree — my best work ever — with it.

A cry twisted through the air. Cassidy was at the top of the driveway, yanking at his leash and howling. I kicked dirt around the fire to keep it from spreading out over the grass.

"Rory, what are you . . . ?"

I caught Dad's face, lit beneath the flood lamp, and stared at him hard. This time I was the one who kept quiet. There was a tight feeling in my stomach, as if a needle were slowly working its way through my insides.

I took one last look at the sketchbook. It lay hidden in the heap of dirt.

I turned and ran into the house. I flew up to my room, threw myself on the bed, and buried my face in the pillow. The picture of the woman appeared, and I shut my eyes tighter to squeeze her away. But the colors just kept swelling, and the harder I pressed, the sharper she got.

at dinner, I pushed the couscous and steamed vegetables around my plate, forming little piles, hoping it would look like I'd eaten something. Once, I looked up and Mom was staring at me with her concerned face.

"Not hungry?" she asked gently.

"Not really." I forced a smile.

Dad kept pushing food onto his fork with a piece of pita bread.

"You don't have to finish," Mom said, her voice full of understanding. Her eyes told me, I know where you are. I remember being there, too.

I wanted to cry for her right then. *You have no idea what monster is sitting next to you, shoveling food into his mouth as if nothing was wrong.*

"I've been thinking about what I want for my birthday." Mom tried to make her voice bright, but I could see that it took more effort than usual.

Dad and I both looked up at her.

"Don't looked so shocked. I know what I said, but maybe turning forty isn't so miserable after all. . . ."

Mom hadn't wanted us to make a big deal over this birthday. No presents. Just something quiet and simple.

A mural can be quiet and simple, I had reasoned.

We had the perfect gift, didn't we, Dad? He wouldn't look at me.

"Nothing too elaborate." She circled her fingers around the rim of her wineglass. "Just something I can look back at when I'm old and say, 'This is what my family gave me to mark the beginning of my mid-life crisis.'" She forced a laugh.

Dad put down his fork and looked at Mom.

She turned her head from him to me. Sadness gathered in the slope of her eyes, and her voice turned soft.

"What if the two artists in the family made me a painting?"

"what's wrong?" Nicky asked the next day in the hall. We were on our way to art. "You seem bummed."

"Nothing."

"You sure?" She cradled her notebook and looked me straight in the eye. "Hello! Like, Earth to Rory."

"Sorry," I said. "I was just thinking."

"About what?"

"About this stupid bra I agreed to wear," I whispered.

She smiled, but there was a glint of suspicion in her face.

"It's itchy," I said. I wanted to tell Nicky about my dad, but it was so embarrassing and painful. How would I find the words to explain it? And I definitely couldn't do it in the hall.

She arched an eyebrow. "Yeah," she said, her voice flat and questioning. "I know what you mean."

Nicky and I had decided that we'd both start wearing a bra, only for her it made sense because she had something to put in it. She started "developing," as Mom called it, last year. But my body couldn't make up its mind. When I looked at myself naked in the mirror, sometimes I saw the fleshy white baby skin of a little girl, and other times I saw real breasts, poking out from my chest, small and unsure.

Nicky and I went to our easels by the window. Next to me, Dean Barnes was drawing pictures of female Power Rangers with big iron-plated boobs.

I looked at him sideways and rolled my eyes. What did Nicky see in him, anyway?

Mr. Miles was handing out clean sheets of paper. Above his desk hung prints by the great painters: Michelangelo, Monet, Picasso, and Georgia O'Keeffe, names and pictures I recognized from my father's art books. A picture of Degas's ballet dancers was there. It was one of my favorites. Dad had said, "When I get my first solo show, we'll go to France and see the real thing." Like we would ever do that now.

On Mr. Miles's desk was a picture of his wife with their two sons. The younger one, who was still a baby, had chocolate ice cream all over his face. I could see Mr. Miles aiming the camera and saying, "Okay, everybody, say ice-cheese," and cracking up.

I'm sure you would never cheat, Mr. Miles. You would never excuse yourself from dinner early, trying to make it seem as though you wanted to get started on

47

a special painting right away when it was so clear to everyone that was a lie.

Mr. Miles was standing back at his easel now, waiting for the class to calm down.

"I have an announcement," he said without raising his voice.

Dean kept drawing. Richie Rodriguez and Aaron Wolfe were in the middle of a thumb-wrestling match. Everyone else was still talking.

"Next week we're all going on a class trip to Disney World."

"For real?" Dean wasn't the brightest kid in seventh grade.

"Right after we return from our exploratory trip to Venus."

Dean looked confused.

"He's kidding," I whispered.

Nicky gave me a weak smile.

"Now that I have your attention," Mr. Miles continued, "I have an important announcement. Hillview is participating in a national art contest with hundreds of other middle schools across the country. First prize is five hundred dollars." He walked around the room and handed us each a small packet. "Every school is allowed to submit three pieces — paintings, drawings, collages, whatever. As you'll see when you read through the material" — he peered up over his glasses at Dean — "and I know you will, the deadline is December twentieth. There will be an exhibition to show all the work and announce the winners right after winter break."

I already knew about the contest. Mr. Miles had stopped me in the hall on the first day of school to tell me about it. "Sure, I'll do it," I'd told him. And when I'd reached my locker and shut my eyes for a minute, a painting began to form. Nothing clear, but the colors were there and the silver rings. Dad was excited when I'd told him about it. "Now's your chance to really shine," he'd said.

"Let me know if you have any questions. Otherwise, I expect that you'll all submit something." Mr. Miles was looking right at me.

I stared at the blank sheet of paper on my easel and then looked out the window.

"Wake up, Rory!" Richie whispered from behind me as he reached over and snapped my bra.

I whipped around and shot him a look. "You're an idiot, Richie." When I turned back around, Mr. Miles was watching us.

"Anything wrong?" he asked.

"Nothing," I said, picking up my pencil and pretending to draw.

He nodded toward me. "Rory, I'd like to see you after class."

Great. Now I was in trouble, too. Nicky looked at me, puzzled. Stupid bra. Why was I wearing it anyway?

I scribbled a note and passed it to Nicky: *It keeps unhooking. I'm taking it off.*

I grabbed the wooden hall pass off the chalkboard ledge and tried to look casual as I walked to the bathroom. Like I wore a bra to school and took it off in the middle of art every day. In the stall, I pulled it through the sleeve of my T-shirt. But now what? If I wrapped it in toilet paper and threw it out, Mom would ask where it was. So I rolled it into a ball and stuffed it into the front pocket of my jeans. I'd just keep one hand in my pocket until science, when I could shove it in my locker.

But Dean must have read the note.

"What's in your pocket, Rory?" he asked as soon as I got back to my easel. "It's not a *bra,* is it?"

"Shut up, Dean," I whispered through my teeth, but by then it was too late. The whole row of boys behind us broke into a fit of laughter.

I shot Nicky a look like "Did you show Dean the note?" because I knew she was jealous that he was my science partner. But she looked back at me and mouthed, "No, I swear."

The bell sounded and people grabbed their things and filed out into the hall. I tried to do the same, but Mr. Miles stopped me.

"Rory . . . ?"

"Oh, yeah, sorry. I forgot."

Nicky stopped in front of us. "Do you want me to wait?"

"Go on, Nicole. She'll catch up," Mr. Miles told her.

I looked down at my sneakers and watched through the corner of my eye as Nicky's Pumas disappeared out the doorway.

"Listen," Mr. Miles started. "You can win this contest."

One of my laces was untied.

"I know it would make your dad proud."

A lump jammed in my throat. "Yeah, whatever."

"Hey, what does that mean?" His voice rose with concern.

"Nothing." I looked up and forced a smile.

"All right. I'll be rooting for you, Rory. But don't tell anyone I said that."

I turned down the empty hallway. *You're wasting your time, Mr. Miles.*

there was a big pot of sauce simmering on the stove when I got home. The living room smelled garlicky and sweet. The barn door was open, and I saw Dad's shadow move across the floor. He was alone.

When he stepped out onto the lawn and started toward the house, I went up to my room.

This morning he had asked, "You want lasagna tonight?" But I didn't answer. Did he really think that cooking my favorite meal could make up for what he'd done? If he thought pretending nothing had happened was going to make the whole thing disappear, he was wrong.

I pulled a book from my knapsack and tried to read. I read the same sentence six times and still couldn't remember it.

Dad tapped the door to my room and looked in. "You want to come to the store? We can have shopping cart races."

I glared at his tall, thin frame in the doorway. "I don't want to play your stupid game," I said. "And besides, I have homework."

He raised an eyebrow and shrugged. Then he started to walk away.

"You could have at least said something about the sketchbook. Like you're sorry it's gone."

"I am," he whispered. More words gathered around his eyes, and a muscle clenched in his throat. He tucked a strand of hair behind his ear and nodded. I could see that he felt bad because something in his face collapsed. But he just shut the door behind him without a sound.

Tears stung my eyes. I threw my book at the wooden dollhouse by the foot of the bed. The furniture clanked inside, and a few pieces tumbled out onto the floor.

"If you were sorry, you wouldn't have wrecked us in the first place. And I'm not forgiving you."

mom's keys made a loud plunk, hitting the table in the entryway.

"Hey, Peter," she called, then her stocking feet padded across the wood floor.

I crept out onto the loft above the living room, where Mom and Dad had set up a small office, and sat in the corner.

"Where's Rory?" Mom asked.

"In her room. She said she had a lot of home-work."

I did not. I didn't say *a lot*.

"Is she okay? She's been so moody and de-pressed lately."

It got quiet.

Are you going to tell her, Dad?

"You haven't noticed?" Mom pressed.

It was silent. I listened for his reply, but Mom's words came first. Dad got away without answering a lot of things this way.

"She goes off, like at dinner last night" — Mom took a breath and unwound the scarf around her neck — "and I just want to grab her and pull her back. But I can't. Sometimes it scares me how alike you two are."

My stomach twisted, and Dad's must have, too, because even through the tiny space between the file cabinet and the desk, I could see his face get stiff.

Orange blotches of color swelled inside my head. The knot in my stomach tightened, like thread pulled too taut through a sweater. Orange was always connected to my stomach.

57

"Did you call about the teaching position?" Mom asked.

"Not yet."

I held my breath, waiting to see how it would turn out this time. Mom was nodding and studying Dad.

"You don't want to do it, do you?" Her voice was gentler than usual.

"It's just —" Dad's words fell off, like stones dropped from a cliff.

"Don't, Peter." Mom picked up her bag and started up the stairs. "I can't hear it anymore."

I went back to my room, picked up the dollhouse furniture, and placed everything neatly in the right rooms. Then I pulled a clean sheet of paper from my bottom desk drawer and sat down. In spite of my anger, I had to try to move forward with the mural — for Mom's sake.

Something I remembered, dislodged from some hidden place inside, was prodding me. I closed my eyes and watched the tree sketch swell up. Like a reliable friend, it came back whole. But other pieces came, too. There was one big splotchy image, painted in yellows and oranges, of the worst fight, almost a year ago, when Mom cried long into the night and then just days and days of silence.

The words she had finally spoken, softly, steadily, pushed me now.

"I want to try, Peter. One last time."

I touched my pencil down and tried to move my hand across the page. But for the first time, it wouldn't go.

I took a breath and tried again. Nothing. My hand sat there stiff and stubborn on the page, like a penny stuck in cement.

I knew then that I had to talk to him. It was clear I needed his help. But I would be firmer this time. I'd make him confess to me what he'd done and swear that it would never happen again. And if he did that, and promised to paint the mural with me, then I would tell him, "Yes, I will keep your secret."

The light was still on in the living room when I woke in the middle of the night and crossed the balcony to the bathroom. The sounds from below were muted, like a painting when there is too much white. But like a small slice of true red cutting through, there was one clear noise. Crying.

A cramp welled up in my side. I got back in bed, but even the darkness beneath the blanket couldn't stop the orange circles from ringing inside my head. I hated hearing them fight. I hated hearing Mom cry.

Cassidy was lying at the foot of my bed. "Come here, boy." I made him put his head on the pillow next to mine. And with my face buried in the ruff of his neck, I must have fallen asleep.

"*why didn't* you wake me?!"

I was standing in the kitchen in my nightgown, screaming and trying to breathe.

Mom reached out a hand to me.

I stepped back. "If you had woken me, I could have made him stay!"

Mom's eyes went dull, like a stray dog who's just been kicked. She stared at me, looking like she wanted to cry, but no tears came. "Maybe you're right," she said, and her voice cracked into little pieces.

61

"It's all your fault! Why couldn't you have tried harder? Then maybe he wouldn't have left. . . ."

I felt like I had scratched her and made her bleed. I didn't even know why I'd said that. It just came out.

"Don't say that, Rory."

"I hate you," I sputtered. "I hate you both." But I knew even as I said them that I didn't mean all these horrible things. Because deep down I was sure it was my fault that my father had left. I was the one who wouldn't talk to him. I'd wanted to punish him for what he did.

Suddenly, I was heaving and gasping and choking on tears.

Mom grabbed my hand and pulled me to her.

"I know," she whispered. "I know."

Part of me wanted to yank away. But she held tight and kept rocking. We stayed that way, folded into each other, soaked with tears. I felt like an old flattened tire, left by the side of the road.

All I did was fall asleep for a few hours and he was gone.

"*don't let* Cass out," I yelled to Mom on Monday morning. "I'll do it." I didn't want to be alone.

"Don't forget to take a key, Rory. I left one on the kitchen table." She came into the doorway of my bedroom, dressed in a pretty blue suit.

I'd never had to think about keys before.

"I've got to go or I'll be late for a meeting." She looked beautiful. Like nothing was wrong.

"You look nice."

"Thanks." She gave me a weak smile and then

rummaged inside her leather bag and pulled out her own keys.

"Do you think he'll call?"

All the prettiness and composure fell away from her, like a wet towel dropped carelessly to the floor. Her lips pinched into a tight zipper and she squeezed her eyes shut for a second. "I don't know, Ror. I don't know anything anymore." She took a breath and ran her long fingers through her hair. "I'll see you tonight. I'll bring pizza."

Dad confessed about the woman. Mom said so yesterday when we talked. Now he was staying at his friend Marcus's apartment in New York City. They had decided it would be best if they separated until they could both sort things out.

Mom tried to remain calm and strong when she told me that what Dad was doing wasn't really about this other woman. But her words were punctured and weak, and I could see that it took every effort to turn them into solid sentences that I might understand. Somehow it all made me feel worse, because here was Mom trying to comfort me, and I couldn't even bring myself to tell her how mean I was to Dad. How I had given him no choice but to go.

If she knew that, would she be mad at me?

Why hadn't I paid better attention? If I had been more understanding, more alert, more careful, I could have done something sooner to keep Dad from leaving.

Cassidy was lying by the front door. He looked up at me without lifting his head from in between his big, black paws as I passed him on my way to the kitchen.

"Come here, Cass." I threw his tennis ball, and when that didn't work, his sock toy. I just wanted to hear the noise he made skidding, nails clicking, across the wooden floors. But he didn't feel like playing.

I forced down a bowl of cereal and stared out the kitchen window. Three soggy Cheerios floated to the top of my bowl. I fished them out and stuck the spoon in my mouth. The milk trudged down my throat like glue.

A blue jay landed on the feeder hanging from the maple. The cracked sunlight created a pattern of woven shadows on the grass below. Warm air drifted in through the screen, smelling like spring even though it was the middle of September. Something about the light reminded me of the leaving time. If Dad were here, drinking his coffee and flipping through the newspaper, he'd agree.

Maybe it was strange, but sometimes when I felt rotten I'd do something to make myself feel even worse. As if too much bad might suddenly turn things good, the way two odd numbers added together always made an even.

That must have been why I took Cassidy into the barn and pulled him onto my lap, all eighty-six pounds of him, and didn't think about being late for school. A few blank canvases leaned against the wall. I saw that the paint box and most of the brushes were gone. Something hollowed out inside me.

My cheek rested on Cassidy's soft head. Our chests rose and fell together as we tried to breathe in the last remaining smells of Dad's paints. Every now and then Cassidy let out a deep sigh.

Or maybe it was me.

"*mondays are* writing days," Ms. Meadow was reminding us in English class. "Ten minutes, as usual." She surveyed our desks to make sure we'd all brought our journals and then sat down at her own desk to write.

The room was very quiet. All you could hear were the soft knocks and whispers of pens and pencils as they glided across paper. My journal was filling with more pictures than words. Seeing them made me miss my sketchbook. I cradled my pencil between my fingers and turned to a blank page.

"This is for your private writing," Ms. Meadow had explained when she told us that part of this year's English class would be keeping a journal. "No one is going to read it but you, so don't worry about what you write or your grammar or spelling or penmanship. This isn't for a grade. It is just for you, to help you get to know yourselves better. Write about your dreams or your fears, something that makes you happy or sad or angry."

I looked over at Nicky who was scribbling away as if this were a timed test. How come she always had so much to say and I didn't? I tried to concentrate on Ms. Meadow's advice: "Just listen to yourself and put it down."

Dear Dad,

Do you remember the time Nicky and I walked into town when we were nine and we each stole a Milky Way bar from the Big Top Candy Store just to see if we could do it? Do you remember how I told you that it was an experiment to see if Mr. Piccolino would notice because he was always falling asleep behind the counter? Plenty of people probably took stuff all the time while he was dozing off, and Nicky and I only took two lousy Milky Ways. They weren't even the big ones, they were fun-size, twenty-five cents each.

But you were mad. You said it didn't matter how much they cost, it was the principle of it. And you made Nicky and me walk back into town and give Mr. Piccolino the money we owed and tell him what we did. You did that, Dad. Do you remember?

I remember because I felt awful. I thought that I was a terrible person and that I had really let you down. On the walk back into town I asked Nicky if she thought you'd still give me drawing lessons. I thought maybe I had broken something that I could never fix.

I know you thought you had to leave Mom and me and that I made you feel that way. I'm *sorry. I shouldn't have done that. And it was wrong of me to barge in on you when you were painting.*

But if you'd tell us that you want to come home and be a family again, then I'd forgive you. I'd forgive you just like you forgave me right when I got back from apologizing to Mr. Piccolino that day, and you told me to hurry up and get my pencils because the light was fading fast.

"Journals away," Ms. Meadow was saying.

When I looked down at the page, it was still blank.

"hey, maidenform Queen!" Richie yelled out from a long Formica table in the cafeteria. I was in line with Nicky, trying to ignore him. His friends were holding their stomachs and howling with laughter.

"Great," I muttered, feeling my face get hot. "Now the whole school knows."

"Ignore them," Nicky said. "They're so immature."

As if her wannabe boyfriend hadn't been the one to start this whole thing. "They'll grow up eventually," she said. Her lips shimmered with frosty-pink lipstick.

"Yeah, whatever." I glanced over my shoulder for just a second.

"Like she needs a bra. Not!" Richie was laughing so hard he pretended to fall backward off the bench.

Dean pushed him all the way off. "Shut up, Richie." He smiled at Nicky, and she actually blushed. I chewed the inside of my cheek until I tasted the warm, metallic blood on my tongue.

"Why are we in line, anyway?" Nicky finally asked. She knew Dad always packed my lunch.

Mom had forgotten to buy the brown lunch bags when she went grocery shopping on Sunday.

"Can't you just pack it in a plastic bag?" she'd asked.

And I wanted to scream, "No! I can't! Because then everyone would know that there's really something wrong here. Don't you see?" But instead I just took the five dollars she'd left on the table with the key.

"My dad's in Philadelphia," I heard myself tell Nicky. "At an exhibition. So there's no food in the house." What was I saying?

"Oh." She stopped looking around the room. "Is something wrong?"

"No, why?" I sawed off a flap of skin inside my cheek.

"You've been acting kind of weird lately."

"Nothing's wrong," but even as I said it, I could see the lie sitting between us like a fat wad of chewed gum.

"Are you sure?"

I felt sick. How could I stand here and lie again to my best friend?

"Hey, Nicky, you want to go outside?" Dean was standing next to us, draping the hood of his jacket over his head.

Nicky gave me a sheepish look, and then because Dean was shifting his feet impatiently, she said, "I'm going, okay?"

Dean started to walk away.

"Meet us out there," Nicky called back before I could answer. She followed Dean through the glass doors out of the cafeteria, while I stayed inside and forced down a rubbery slice of pizza by myself.

"*rory!*" a voice called from down the hall at the end of the day. "Can I talk to you for a minute?" Mr. Miles was weaving his way through the crowded corridor. Nicky was across the hall, showing Dean her new Rollerblades.

I'm going to tell her on our way home.

"Listen," Mr. Miles said when he finally reached my locker. "I wanted to let you know that I'm keeping the art room open after school until the contest deadline. So if you want extra time to work on your painting. . . ."

"I'm sorry, Mr. Miles, but I can't."

"I know your dad's got that great studio at home, but I thought just in case you wanted to —"

"I can't do the contest."

"What do you mean?"

"It's not possible."

"Not possible?"

I looked down at my sneakers. I hated myself for what I was about to say. "It's just that I'm really busy with a painting my dad and I are working on. For my mom's birthday. And he needs me to come home right away after school and work on it so it will be ready in time."

Mr. Miles just stood there. I could feel him studying me. "What about during class? You can work on it then."

"Yeah, but we're so focused on my mom's painting, I'm kind of burnt on ideas."

"I can help you with an idea if that's the problem." His voice was so gentle it made my insides shrivel.

"Uh-huh."

Please just leave it alone, Mr. Miles.

I looked up at him and he fixed me so hard with his gaze that I couldn't move. I tried to swallow back the tightness in my throat.

"The door's always open, Rory."

"I already told you I can't."

"To talk." He turned away and then back for a second. "You can talk to me."

I grabbed my jacket, pulled my knapsack from the locker, and turned to get Nicky. But by the time I had gathered all my stuff, she and Dean were already disappearing down the hallway. My stomach twisted. Is that what she meant about having a boyfriend? That we weren't going to be friends anymore?

i pulled the latch on the mailbox and fanned through the stack of letters: an electricity bill, a *New York Times* renewal notice, a bank statement, and *Bon Appetit* magazine. The white mailing label on the magazine was the one thing addressed to my father: Peter Forrester, 1030 Crescent Drive, Hillview, New York 10522. Something sunk inside my stomach.

I shoved the magazine back in the mailbox with the few other pieces of junk mail that had come to him. That's when something came unstuck from the back of the magazine. The envelope tumbled out and landed on my foot.

I recognized the strong block print right away, in all capital letters: RORY FORRESTER. Suddenly it was as if he were standing in the yard with me.

I took it to the tree stump to read it. I was careful not to tear the envelope or rip the place where he had written his name. In small, square letters on the back it said: *P. Forrester, 121 Flatbush Avenue, Brooklyn, NY 11217.*

Dear Rory,

The picture on this card is a Leonardo. See how much light he brings in with just a pencil? I knew you would appreciate it. Do you remember that the shading is called chiaroscuro? And that in Italian, it means "clear dark?"

I'm sitting in Marcus's kitchen, which is also the living room, dining room, and bedroom. He leaves next week for Germany, so I'll have the place to myself for three months while he mounts a show in Berlin. Too bad it's not me having the show. I could really use that right now.

It's one open space here, kind of like my studio at home, only smaller. But it has good light and a great rooftop. I can see the Empire State Building from up there, and on a good, clear day, if I squint, I can even make out the Statue of Liberty.

I'm working on a new painting — a landscape of houses pressed into a steep hillside. I don't know why I'm so drawn to these houses. Maybe because on my canvases they give me a sense of stability that I can never have in my real life. I wish it weren't that way. I know this probably doesn't make any sense to you, Rory, but one day you'll understand.

Someday, when you're older, you may also need to make yourself a leaf in the breeze, tossing yourself just to see where you end up.

*I miss you. I'll write more soon. Give Cass
a hug for me.*

Love, Dad

It had been two weeks without a single word
from him. Long enough to make the wishing place
inside me go numb. I read the letter again, and then
a third time, hoping that I had somehow just missed
the part about him coming back.

I studied the rings on the tree stump and
rubbed at the knot in my side. I used to draw for
hours by this spot, without even noticing the time
passing. Mom said I was just like Dad, the way I
could lose myself.

Once, in summer, I went out after breakfast and
sketched until Mom's car drove up the long, steep
driveway at the end of the day. I drew straight
through lunch without ever feeling hungry. Time
must have seemed like the wind then, blowing by.
But not anymore. Not when you were waiting and
you didn't even know what for.

It had rained and the stump was damp. Its brown rings were vivid and dark. I could make out every line. Dad showed me that you can tell how old a tree is by counting the rings in its trunk — one ring for each year. A few of them were very thick, and others were as thin as a needle. I guess there are some years when time moves faster than others.

The rich color of the wood made me feel like drawing. The mural was still hanging on in my mind, like a stubborn weed that pushes itself up through a crack of concrete. I closed my eyes for a minute and tried to get a clearer image. But just as I was about to pull a pencil from my knapsack, a cramp bit through my hand.

nicky called later that night. She wanted to know how the mural was going.

"Not that great," I admitted.

"So I guess you'll need to work extra hard. I mean, your mom's birthday is pretty soon, right?"

"Yeah." *Yeah to the second part* is what I should have said, but I had knotted myself up in so many lies, I didn't know where to begin untangling. What if I told her and she blabbed it to Dean? Then the whole school would find out that my dad was a cheater. And that my mom and I weren't worth loving.

"You should hang out with Dean and me after school sometime." There was excitement licking at the edges of Nicky's voice.

"Maybe when we finish," I said, but I was thinking that it used to be just the two of us. She didn't even ask what I thought about Dean.

I could hear Jonah and Mrs. Abrams laughing in the background. Their house always seemed to be filled with laughter and talk.

"Well, I guess we should go," she said.

"I guess," I told her, not wanting to hang up.

"See you tomorrow?"

"Sure." My dinner shifted in my stomach.

"'Bye," she said.

I listened to the hollow click before the line went dead.

sometime during the next few weeks, Nicky and I stopped walking home from school together completely.

"Rory, come to Mr. Miles's room with us," she said one afternoon from her perch by Dean's locker across the hall. They were both working on paintings for the art contest.

"I can't."

"Please. I need your input. Dean says my painting looks like a gorilla eating a giant chicken bone, and it's supposed to be a girl playing the guitar."

I managed a smile, but then gave her a knowing look that said, "The mural, remember?" I knew she was only offering to be nice. She didn't need me anymore. Not like she used to.

So I'd take Cassidy down to the river to sit on our rock and smell the water and watch the birds looping over the waves. Sometimes I brought my letters from Dad and reread them. There were three now, and not one of them directly answered the one from English class that I'd finally written down and sent.

I was halfway across the bridge over the train tracks one Friday afternoon when I saw Nicky and Dean on the jetty, skipping rocks into the gray-green water. Cassidy barked and tugged on his leash. "Quit it, Cass," I said, stopping, and snapping the leash harder than I meant to.

"Hey, Rory!" Nicky had spotted us and was waving us over.

Part of me wanted to turn around and run back home, but Cassidy and I climbed down the stone steps and over the big rocks to where they stood, close to each other. So close the sleeves of their jackets were touching.

"I thought you and your dad were working." Nicky palmed a flat rock in her hand and then gave it to me.

"Yeah," Dean said. "Your mural sounds really cool." The wind seemed to gather his words, pack them tight, and send them sailing like a snowball straight at my face.

I looked at Nicky. *You told him?* Tears sprung into the corners of my eyes. Quickly, I moved to the edge of the jetty and threw the rock sidearm into the water. I picked up more rocks and hurled them one after the other, their sides skimming the surface two, three, four times before they sunk beneath the dark waves.

Nicky followed me to the edge. "What is up with you?"

I kept tossing rocks. They made a *jeet, jeet, plunk* sound that echoed in the quiet between us.

"Rory, I don't get you anymore. What did I do?"

I turned to her. "The mural was supposed to be a secret." It was hard to tell who was more surprised by the sharpness of my voice.

Nicky's mouth formed a small O, but I didn't wait for her to answer. I grabbed Cassidy and pulled him back over the rocks and across the bridge.

How could my best friend suddenly give away my secrets, as if they were a bunch of outgrown clothes?

"anybody call?" Mom asked when she came home that night.

Cassidy and I were lying on the sofa, watching the *Real World* on MTV.

"Aunt Carol."

"Oh, God, I completely forgot to call her back last night." Mom unpacked small white cardboard containers of Chinese food onto the kitchen table behind me. We had been eating takeout for the past three weeks. Or at least I was. Mom just picked at her food lately. She looked thin.

"She said she'll be here by noon tomorrow." I turned back to the TV screen where Pedro was yelling at Puck for sticking his fingers in the peanut butter jar.

"No one else?"

"Still no."

Mom blew a bubble of air into her cheeks, then let it out. "I'm sorry, honey."

"Whatever."

Dad still hadn't called. Mom knew about the letters. "You can read them," I'd said because I saw a wing of sadness flutter in her eyes. But she just shook her head and, in a voice that was a little too cheerful, said, "No, they're for you."

"Do you think I should call him?" I'd asked. "You know how he hates the phone."

"He could make the effort. Just because he and I aren't talking right now doesn't mean he can't call you." Her voice had rattled like our old radiator, and I think she was a little surprised by the tone of it, because she took a long, slow breath and steadied herself. "I just think he owes you that much. But you should do whatever you need to do."

Maybe she was right.

"What's going on in school?" Mom asked and folded the brown bag and stuck it in the cabinet.

"Nothing."

"Any cute boys?" She was starting to sound like Nicky.

"No."

"Not even the eighth graders?" Mom kept talking to the back of my head. "I remember when I started junior high. There was this guy Tommy —"

"Could you stop?"

Mom looked up, her eyes unblinking. "I'm just trying to make things normal."

"I know," I said. "But it's making it worse." I went back to watching Pedro and Puck who were trying to get their roommates to take sides.

Mom came around the sofa, picked up the remote, and clicked off the TV. She repositioned the blanket around my legs and sat down. "You're so quiet all the time. You never used to watch this much TV. And I can't remember the last time I saw you pick up your sketchbook. Are you sure you don't want to talk?"

"What's there to say?"

A tear escaped down my cheek. I hated that. Why did everything make me cry lately?

Mom wiped away the tear. "I don't mean to push you, honey. I know you need time. But you've got to talk to someone. And I'm not sure Nicky knows the right questions to ask. Do you want me to call the guidance counselor at school and set something up?"

"No!" Everyone knew the kinds of kids who emerged, heads bent into their jackets, from Ms. Leibowitz's green office with the mustard-colored plastic chairs. Lorette Patrick whose brother was killed in a drunk-driving accident. Jesse Summers who was anorexic. Aaron Wolfe whose dad was once in jail. "I'm not doing that."

"It was just an idea."

I don't even have Nicky anymore, I thought, and another tear fell down my cheek. Dark, murky blotches of color swelled inside my head.

"Why don't you talk about him?" I asked.

"I guess I don't want to load you down with more stuff than you're already dealing with."

"I can handle it."

Mom curled a strand of hair around my ear. "I know. I don't want to take advantage of that."

"It feels weird your not talking about it."

Mom nodded. "I didn't realize that. But I'm glad you told me. I'll work on it." She smiled and squeezed my hand. "We're both going to get through this."

I wished she sounded more convinced.

The phone rang while we were eating dinner.

"It's Nicky," Mom said, pulling the phone cord across the table.

I shook my head, and Mom gave me a slow, queer look before telling Nicky that I'd call her later. Mom wouldn't take her eyes off me for the rest of the meal.

"I'm fine," I said. "I just don't feel like talking."

"*oh, pooker,* what'd you do that for?" Mom said when she opened the door and found Aunt Carol draped in colorful packages. Pooker was Aunt Carol's childhood nickname, and she wasn't my real aunt. She was Mom's best friend since they were kids.

Aunt Carol smiled under her floppy black hat. "It's cold as Iceland up here." She shivered. "Now I know why George and I never leave the city."

Mom laughed and held the door open for her. "Come on, we've got a fire going."

I was holding Cassidy to keep him from leaping out the door and jumping all over Aunt Carol.

"Aurora Borealis! Hey, girl." She kissed my cheek and gave me a good, hard squeeze. Aunt Carol had a million names for me, but that was my favorite. "You're one of a kind, kid," she always said. "Just like those northern lights."

Cassidy nuzzled himself between our legs until Aunt Carol bent to pet him.

She wiggled out of her coat and gave it to me to hang in the hall closet. "How's my favorite girl?" she asked. Her cheer filled the house.

"I'm fine."

"I've missed you guys." She kicked off her big black boots and pulled off her hat. Her smooth dark hair was cut tight and cropped. Static electricity made a few strands at the crown of her head stand straight up on end. Aunt Carol had a face like a fawn, narrow and delicate, with enormous brown eyes and a small, almost fragile red mouth. There was a soft glow around her all the time.

"I know, it's been too long, Pook," Mom said, apologetic, as she wrapped her arms around Aunt Carol's shoulders.

"My God, Maddy, you're skin and bone," Aunt Carol said as she ran her hands up and down Mom's arms.

Mom smiled weakly.

"Maybe she'll listen to you," I said.

"Okay, you two." Mom waved away our comments and motioned with her chin toward the living room. "Go sit by the fire and warm up. Rory, why don't you open these presents that your crazy aunt shouldn't have gotten us. I'll make some tea."

Mom's voice sounded smoother and surer with Aunt Carol here, the way it used to sound.

Cassidy followed Aunt Carol to the sofa and started licking her thick purple socks that peeked out from under her black gauzy skirt. She bent over to kiss his head. I flopped down next to her.

"What's going on with you, Rory Bory? You okay?"

The way she said it, I knew she was referring to Dad.

I shrugged.

"It really stinks, doesn't it? My parents got divorced when I was ten."

Mom had told me that.

"They used to scream at each other, slam doors, throw things. It was a circus most of the time. So when they finally decided to split, it was kind of a relief. But I was miserable anyway. I don't know what I would have done without your mom. I practically lived at her house." She cupped Cassidy's ears in her hands and scratched. He let out a happy moan. "At least your parents love each other."

"They don't anymore."

"Yeah, they do, honey. Sometimes people can love each other and still not be able to live together."

"That doesn't make much sense. If you love each other, you should try."

"You're right. But if only one person wants to try, it's not enough." Aunt Carol slipped her fingers in and out of mine. "Go easy on her, okay? She's having a rough time of it."

Mom poked her head around from the corner of the kitchen and held up the colorful tea boxes. "Cranberry Cove, Ginger, or Jasmine — take your pick."

"Ginger for me."

"Me, too," I said.

Mom carried in a tray with a teapot and three big mugs. Along with some books and scented candles, one of the presents Aunt Carol had brought us was homemade chocolate chip cookies, and we munched on those with our tea. The afternoon curled away while we sat around and talked.

"Sometimes I think Rory and I are better off without him." Mom frowned.

Something in my face must have fallen because when Mom looked up, she reached out a hand to me even though she was too far away to touch me. "I'm sorry, honey. I shouldn't have said that. I'm just —"

"It's okay. I want to hear."

Aunt Carol massaged the back of my neck. "You need a vacation, Maddy."

"Tell me about it." Mom pulled her hair back from her face.

"Hey, why don't you come to Puerto Rico with George and me at the end of December?"

"Oh, please, Pooker. I can't."

"Why not? George is going to be working most of the time anyway. He's shooting a travel video on the rain forest. And we've got an apartment right on the beach, all paid for. The only thing you'd have to take care of is the flight."

"I don't know," Mom said.

"Come on, Maddy. You need this. And besides, I could use the company."

"We'll see," she said, as if she really were weighing the thought.

Mom wasn't going to take off, was she?

I smiled for Aunt Carol's sake and then picked up the tray of empty mugs. "I'll make more tea."

From the kitchen, I could hear their voices swirling through the house. Mom wouldn't just go and leave like Dad. But something about the idea got under my skin.

Seeing Mom and Aunt Carol together made me happy and sad all at once. I was glad that Mom was livelier than she'd been in a long time, but the way she and Aunt Carol were so close they could practically read each other's minds made me miss Nicky so much I could die.

I lit the burner beneath the kettle and waited for it to hiss.

"Aren't you joining us?" Aunt Carol asked when I set the tray, with only two mugs, back down.

"I think I'm going to go over to Nicky's for a while."

"Sure, honey." Mom gave me an approving smile.

"Take some cookies!" Aunt Carol exclaimed. "I must have made about a hundred."

"And be back for dinner. Carol's cooking."

I took the cookies back to the kitchen to wrap them.

Maybe if I could explain to Nicky about Dad, she would see how much I needed her now and break up with Dean.

red leaves twirled in the crisp autumn air. I collected the prettiest ones, gathered them like a bouquet, and carried them, along with the plate of cookies, to the Abrams' house.

When I tapped the kitchen door, Jonah opened it.

"Hey, Michelangelo. Haven't seen you for a while." He shut the door behind me and sat back down on the high stool. A family of pots and pans hung above his head, and *Rolling Stone* magazine was open in front of him on the wooden island in the middle of the kitchen. "Where've you been?"

I set the cookies on the table but held onto the leaves. They were for Nicky. "Around."

Jonah eyed the cookies and rubbed his hands together. "Are those for me?"

"They're for everyone. My aunt made them."

"Thanks." Jonah peeled back the plastic wrap and bit into a cookie.

"Is Nicky around?"

He shook his head and the small silver hoop earring in his left ear glittered against his auburn hair. "She and my mom are checking out decorations for the New Year's party. They'll be home soon, if you want to wait."

It was quiet for a moment, and then the kitchen door handle wriggled.

"Great," Jonah muttered as Sam came through the door.

"Hey, dude." Sam's voice was raspy. Jonah didn't answer him. He just bent his head into the magazine.

"What's up, Rory?" Sam was even more hand-some than Jonah with full red lips and copper curls that fell just above his shoulders. He was wearing a dark blue hooded sweatshirt that said STATE in blocky white letters.

"Nothing," I said and suddenly felt shy.

"Dude. Where'd the cookies come from?"

Before I could even answer, he was on them like a hawk. "Cool, man, I'm starving." He popped one in his mouth, and then another. He devoured two more and reached for a fifth.

Jonah peered up over his magazine. "They're for everyone."

"D'you say something, man?" Sam's eyes were squinty and rimmed with pink.

"Nothing, Sam." Jonah watched him grab a fistful. "Relax," he whispered.

Then Sam's blue sweatshirt disappeared into the living room, and his heavy footsteps pounded on the stairs to the basement. In a minute the floor was vibrating from his drums.

"He's such an idiot," Jonah muttered into the magazine.

"He looked like he was crying."

Jonah almost laughed. "Yeah, right. Real big ganja tears."

I must have looked confused.

"Didn't Nicky tell you?"

"Tell me what?"

"Sam got suspended for getting high on school property. He can kiss that soccer scholarship good-bye."

"I'm sorry." I brushed the tips of the leaves across my palm. I didn't know what else to say.

"My mom says it's because everything comes too easy for him."

"When did it happen?"

"About two weeks ago. He's on probation now. You can see how seriously he's taking it."

Why didn't Nicky tell me?

And then, like an old television snapping into focus, everything became clear. I was the one who had started the secret keeping, holding my breath, afraid to let it out. At first, it was just a week. But then one week became two and three, until I didn't notice anymore that I had stopped breathing, that something had gone dead inside me — and the secret had killed it.

I had shut myself off from Nicky — just like my father was doing to me. I felt my throat begin to close.

"I gotta go," I told Jonah.

He looked puzzled. "They should be home soon."

"I can't," I managed as I pushed the door open and raced out before he could see my tears. I threw the leaves into the wind, their red bodies shaking before they hit the ground.

"what happened?" Mom asked when I got home. "Nicky called a minute ago. You guys must have just missed each other."

"Yeah," I said, peeling off my jacket and joining Mom and Aunt Carol in the kitchen. The house smelled thick with spices. It reminded me of Dad.

"You want to help?" Aunt Carol tossed salt and pepper into the big silver pot on the stove and stirred.

Louis Armstrong and Ella Fitzgerald were singing on the stereo, their voices strong and *109* joyful. Mom and Aunt Carol were drinking wine and singing along.

"Sure."

"I invited Nicky for dinner," Mom said.

I felt my heart do a somersault. "Is she coming?"

"She's on her way."

"Maybe I should take Cass out before —"

"I'll do it," Aunt Carol offered. "Your friend will be here any minute. Here, stir the sauce for me." She passed me the wooden spoon.

Beside me, Mom was washing lettuce in the sink, singing softly, and swaying her hips from side to side.

When the front door opened, I heard Aunt Carol say, "Hi, Nicky. Come on in. They're in the kitchen. Cass and I will be right back."

Nicky came around the corner.

"*Hola, chica,*" Mom said. "*¿Que pasa?*"

"I'm fine." It wasn't like Nicky not to answer in Spanish.

"You want something to drink?" I asked and

she nodded.

"How're your parents?" Mom asked.

"They're good." Nicky hugged the counter behind her.

"Sam must be applying to college already."

I stuck my head in the refrigerator. "Mom, where's the Coke?" I said, maybe a little too loudly.

She craned her head around. "It's right there on the top shelf."

"Oh, yeah, duh." I grabbed it and poured Nicky a glass.

"Ror, the sauce is starting to bubble." Mom nudged her chin toward the pot. "Nicky, hon, you want to set the table?"

"Okay." I watched as she opened the cabinets, pulled down five plates, and started toward the table. The whole thing seemed to unfold in slow motion, but I still couldn't stop it.

"You guys invite someone else?" Mom asked.

Nicky looked at me confused. "Isn't your aunt staying for dinner?"

I felt sick.

"She is." Mom's voice trailed off at the end, and she turned to me with big questions in her eyes. Her eyebrows raised themselves into hard, concerned points.

It hurt to look at her.

"Mr. Forrester won't be home for dinner," Mom told Nicky, slowly, evenly, with layers of sadness woven into each word. She wouldn't take her eyes off me.

Nicky put back a plate.

Mom kept staring at me until I couldn't look at her anymore.

"Why don't you guys go hang out for a while," she said, her voice kind. "Dinner won't be ready for almost an hour. I'll finish up the table, Nicky."

There was a rising in my chest as we climbed the stairs to my room in silence. I shut the door and sat down next to Nicky on the floor.

"What's going on, Rory?" Her voice was warm. "Did I do something?"

I shook my head.

"I'm sorry about the mural. It was dumb of me to tell Dean, but I just felt proud of you." She spoke so gently it made me feel like even more of a heel. "Why aren't you talking to me?"

"My dad —" I started and then a vice clamped in my throat. Nicky's eyes seemed to pull the words out of me. "He left. That's why we only needed four plates. He and my mom are probably getting divorced because he cheated on her." I stopped to take a breath and to check Nicky's expression. It was surprised but open.

"That's awful." Her face crumpled and I thought she might start crying, too. "I'm really sorry. I can't believe he did that."

"I should have told you. It just hurts so much to talk about it."

Nicky moved closer and put her arm around my shoulder. "I knew something was up," she said quietly. "I just wish I'd made you talk to me sooner."

"There's no mural, either," I told her. "I've been lying about that, too. I haven't even felt like drawing since he left — since September."

"You haven't drawn for that long?" Nicky looked at me, disbelieving.

I shook my head. "I miss it so much."

"Why aren't you?"

"I can't — not without him."

"You should try, Rory. You're not you if you don't draw."

I let her words sink in while we sat in silence. It didn't feel weird at all.

"There's stuff going on in my family, too," Nicky confessed after a few minutes.

"I know. Jonah told me."

"About Sam?"

I nodded.

"My dad's been threatening to kick him out of the house." Nicky's eyes went wide. "Where would he go?"

It got quiet again. Downstairs, the door opened,

and I could hear the jangle of Cassidy's leash against the wood floor.

"I hate not talking to you," I said.

"Me, too. Hanging out with Dean definitely isn't the same."

Inside, I felt myself backing away at the sound of his name.

"I know he says stupid stuff sometimes, but he's pretty funny and nice."

I was moving farther and farther away. Why couldn't I be funny?

"He's not you, though. And mostly I just hang out with him because you're not around."

"Really?"

Nicky nodded. "I would never invite him to Paris. He just wouldn't appreciate it."

A peculiar sound came out of me that was half laugh and half sniffle. "You better not."

And then we were both silent again.

"Do you remember when I jumped out of the tree and sprained my thumb?" Nicky asked.

"You didn't talk to me for three whole days because I laughed at your splint."

"Do you remember what you said when I finally came over?"

I thought for a minute, but I couldn't remember.

"You said best friends talk to each other when something's wrong; that's part of what makes them bests. Otherwise, they're just regular friends. And then you asked me if I wanted to be regular friends or best friends."

"I said that?" I asked, feeling a bit proud of myself.

Nicky nodded.

"What did you answer?"

"Well, of course —" Nicky began, and then she saw me smiling and started tickling me in all my worst spots.

"Uncle!" I cried.

Nicky stopped tickling and her face turned serious. "No more secrets. We have to promise."

"I promise," I told her, hooking my pinky around hers. And I knew I really meant it. No more lying to my best friend.

Then Nicky whispered something in Dog Latin, "I-day of-de-lay oo-de-yay."

"Me, too," I said, because translated it meant, "I love you."

by the end of November, winter already felt endless, like a long stretch of highway that never seemed to meet the horizon — the closer you got, the more you saw the flat curve of blacktop laid out before you. And it was cold. It had snowed three times at least, big snows. Mom and I had both worked our backs shoveling the long, steep driveway, until every muscle had screamed for us to stop.

Mr. Miles had finally stopped bugging me

about the contest. As much as I dreaded his prodding, the silence of his letting go was worse.

There were a few more letters from Dad, but still no phone calls.

On Mom's birthday, a huge bouquet of flowers arrived. I think we both hoped for a moment that they were from Dad. But the tiny card announced that it was Nana who'd sent them and she was sorry she couldn't be here to celebrate. We'd known for a while that she would be away on a cruise. I made French toast and fried bananas for breakfast and set the table with Mom's favorite printed tablecloth and served orange juice in champagne glasses.

"It's beautiful, Rory," she said when she opened my present and held the long icy-blue-and-lilac scarf up to her face. "You have such good taste."

Beautiful, but not the one present you asked for.

The day before, while I had wrapped her present in my room, I watched out the window as she returned from walking Cassidy. Before they came back inside, Mom went over to the barn; and then she did something strange. She patted the door like it was Cassidy's soft fur. Her hand stroked the knobby red wood, and her whole body fell against it, as if she would have just melted into the ground were the barn not there to catch her. In that moment, more than ever, I wished I could have given her the mural myself, but I couldn't.

That night it snowed again, and water leaked through the skylight into the living room. Mom started to cry.

"I'll call Mr. Abrams," I told her. "He'll come fix it." She just sat there, staring up.

"I don't want him to fix it," she said, and a fat tear dripped into her mouth.

Cassidy let out a short moan and nudged his chin onto her lap. Lately, anything could make Mom get weepy, and I was used to it.

"When we first moved in, your father said there wasn't enough light coming in," she said. "So he took off most of the roof and put in skylights, seven of them."

I climbed onto the sofa beside her, fitting myself into the curve of her body like a missing puzzle piece.

"I was eight months pregnant with you and worried that you'd be born shivering because he had left a big hole in the center of the living room. It snowed inside for nearly a week before he would acknowledge that the job was too big for him.

"'A little cold air won't hurt the baby,' he'd said. 'Besides, she'll be grateful for all the sunlight.'

"Five weeks later, when you were born, the hole was gone, and the biggest skylight of all was in your room. The light poured in, thick like fog lifting off the river. You were the warmest baby ever."

I looked up and saw tears rolling down her cheeks.

"He was the one who thought of the name Aurora." When her voice cracked, I lifted my arms over her head and steadied her. "Because on the morning you were born, it dawned the most beautiful pink we had ever seen."

It was quiet after that, except for the drops of water trickling in from the skylight.

The two of us just sat there, and I held Mom tight and let her cry.

a few weeks later, the black suitcase lay wide open on Mom's bed and she was pitching underwear into it, carelessly.

I fingered the blue-and-yellow-plaid pillow while she contemplated a high shelf stacked with cotton sweaters.

"Can't I go?" I bit down on a flap of loose skin inside my cheek, knowing what she'd say.

"Honey, we've talked about this. You know we can't afford two airline tickets right now." She stopped for a minute to cradle my chin in her hand. *123*

"I really need this trip. And Aunt Carol is making that possible. Please try to understand. I know this is hard on you, too, but try. I've got to find some peace of mind."

Mom opened a dresser drawer and started tossing T-shirts onto the bed. "Besides, you and Nana will have fun."

"I'm not a baby. Please don't try to convince me that staying in some stuffy apartment while you're lying on a beach is going to be fun."

Even Nicky would be on the beach. She and her family were going to visit her grandparents in Florida.

Mom stopped packing. She turned around and came over to sit on the bed next to me. "You're right," she said and held my elbows. "It's not fair. And I'm sorry. But could you let me do this?"

"Why?"

"Because I'm tired all the time. I'm missing my deadlines at work. I'm constantly forgetting things." She took a breath. "I've missed my stop on the train twice in the past week because I fell asleep."

"When Dad was here, we always went away together." My voice was very small.

"It's only for four days, honey. I'll be home before you know it."

I wiggled my finger into a hole in my sock. Why did everybody I cared about have to leave?

Mom tilted my chin up and made me look at her. Small pillows of exhaustion puffed beneath her eyes. "Is this really too hard for you? Because if it is, I won't go."

I shook my head.

"Are you sure?"

I shook my head again. But inside, I knew I had to let her go. Maybe in Puerto Rico she could find the piece of her mind that was missing.

early in the morning, Mom scurried around the house like a worker ant. She pulled the plugs on the coffeemaker, the television, and the answering machine. She drew all the window shades and checked the oven knobs at least three times.

"Rory, double-check the basement door, will you?" she said, filling the watering can in the kitchen sink.

I knew Cassidy sensed something was up because he pawed me and licked my hands anytime I was still.

"Can't he come?" I'd asked one last time that morning.

"Rory, please. You know it would be too much for Nana. Mrs. Morris will be here twice a day to walk and feed him."

Mrs. Morris was our veterinarian's assistant. "But Cass cries every time he sees her," I tried. It didn't work.

Cassidy followed me downstairs, and the phone rang. It was Mr. Miles. What was he doing calling me at home?

"I'm going through all the paintings for the contest," he said. "It's killing me, Rory, that there isn't one from you. It's just not right. I'm wondering if you might reconsider. I could give you till the end of the week."

Through the glass door leading out to the yard, I watched Mom struggle with the giant chain lock on the barn door.

"We're going on vacation," I told him. "I won't be back until school starts in January."

There was silence. "I could give you my address, if you want to mail me something, a pencil drawing maybe."

"I'm sorry," I told him before hanging up, and I really was.

"Oh, wait!" Mom said as the taxi pulled up at 88th Street and Central Park West. "I almost forgot." She pulled a book from her bag. "I'm sorry I didn't have time to wrap it. I know you haven't felt like drawing lately, but I hope you'll change your mind."

She handed me a brand-new black sketchbook.

A wave of guilt rolled through me. I knew I'd never use it.

"Try," she said. "I think you'll feel better if you do."

I nodded.

"Please try not to be mad at me," she said.

"I'm not mad." I managed a smile. But part of me was still hoping that she'd say, "Why don't you just come along? We'll find the money somehow."

Mom cupped the back of my head and pulled me close. "I'll miss you," she said into my hair. "Now go, before I change my mind about leaving."

The bologna-colored wallpaper that lined the halls in Nana's building made me feel pukish. Nana's door was already ajar when I reached the apartment.

"Aurora!" She took my cheeks in both hands. "Mmm. You get more beautiful every time I see you." She kissed my neck. "Delicious!"

"Hi, Nana."

"Hi yourself. Where's your mother?"

"She's in a rush. She said to tell you we'll visit on Sunday."

"No time for a quick hello?" Nana raised a wiry eyebrow, but then quickly waved away the disappointment. "C'mon, let's get you squared away."

Since there was no official guest room, and no dresser with real drawers, I unpacked piles of clothes onto the cushioned bench beside the television in the den. Clean sheets and a mustard afghan were stacked on the arm of the sofa. A fat dish of sticky sour balls in every color sat on the end table beside the fisherman lamp and the photo of Grampa. It smelled wrong in here, like milk that had turned.

In the kitchen, Nana had a big pot of soup on the stove. I took the wooden spoon and slid it through the golden broth while she plucked more items from the refrigerator.

"How is it?"

"Fine," I said, sipping at a small puddle on the spoon.

"And how are you? Your mother tells me your father hasn't even called you." Her voice tipped up at the end, disapprovingly. Or maybe she was just hoping it wasn't true. It was hard to tell with Nana. "She means well," Mom had said. "But sometimes it just comes out wrong."

"He hates the phone." I realized how lame that sounded even before Nana turned a pained face toward me.

130 "That's hardly a reason." She tried to hug me,

but I felt my arms stiffen inside her hands. Nana let go. "Let's take a walk," she said quickly and put out the light beneath the soup.

We wandered down Fifth Avenue and looked at the windows all dressed up for Christmas. Nana chattered the whole time, and I was relieved not to have to talk. When we passed a fancy art supply store near Saks, she stopped to peer in. It looked nothing like Pearl Paint in Chinatown where Dad sometimes took me. Pearl was huge and messy like someone's studio, and it smelled of turpentine and sawdust. You could just tell that all the people who worked there were artists because they knew so much about the different glues and papers and brushes.

"Let's go in." Nana ushered me through the glass door before I could protest.

It was warm inside and a cinnamon-and-clove scent filled the small, square room. The shelves were neatly lined with handmade paper and inkwells *131* and calligraphy pens. A few gold frames and leather-bound journals were mixed in among woodcut letter holders and an array of metal stamps.

"Can I help you find something?" The man was tall and thin. A tightly trimmed goatee framed his mouth, and there were two small points with almost no hair at the corners of his lips.

"Do you have any paint sets?" Nana asked, lifting her glasses to scan the shelf behind him.

"As a matter of fact, we just received a lovely watercolor set." He slid a key into a glass case and pulled a wooden box from the bottom shelf. He opened it on top of the counter for us.

"Ooooh, Rory, it's beautiful."

Inside, tiny eggs of color sat in perfect oval carved beds. It looked like an Easter basket filled with shiny tinsel-wrapped chocolates in every color — cherry red, ripe lime green, juicy plum. My mouth must have fallen open.

"We'll take it!" Nana exclaimed.

"But, Nana —"

"How often do I get to spoil you like this?" She smiled and pulled her wallet from her purse.

The antique cash register was jingling and Nana was already handing over her credit card before I could tell her that I wasn't painting anymore. And anyway, Dad and I painted in acrylics. I had never used watercolors in my life.

nana kept me busy. We saw *Cats* on Broadway and watched the skaters at Rockefeller Center and spent an entire afternoon at the Museum of Natural History.

I was so tired by the time we got home from the museum, it was all I could do to eat dinner and make it through two sitcoms.

Nana came into the living room and handed me a mug of hot chocolate. Her fat photo album lay open on my lap.

"That was our honeymoon on Miami Beach."

She leaned over my shoulder. Grampa was dark and muscley. Nana looked like a little bird perched on his thick shoulders.

In another picture they were sipping icy drinks on lounge chairs by a pool. I turned a few pages, and then suddenly my mother appeared, a tiny bundle wrapped against the cold. Nana looked tired but happy.

"We had just come home from the hospital. Leave it to your mother to arrive during a snowstorm."

It was funny seeing Mom so little and frail.

As I turned the pages, Mom grew bigger. There was a picture of her in a blue bikini with yellow-and-white daisies on it, digging sand at the beach; another of her in a mint-green Girl Scout uniform where her skinny calves and big feet made it look like she had two spoons for legs; and one of Mom and Aunt Carol dressed for the prom in candy-colored gowns.

Finally, I stopped at a picture of Mom and Dad

at their wedding. Dad looked funny in a suit, as though it was borrowed from someone much smaller than him. He was smiling at the camera, and Mom was smiling up at him. She looked so beautiful, with her hair swept up like an old movie actress. There was no yellow in her eyes.

"I knew even then it wouldn't work. He was too much in his own world." Nana clicked her tongue. "I could have predicted this."

Orange blotches of color welled up inside my head. How could she say that? She sounded proud of herself for being right.

"I'm tired." I closed the book and went back to the den and fell on the sofa.

Dad was not in his own world. Not always anyway.

Nana didn't know what she was talking about.

"*i'm going* to stay here," I told Nana at breakfast.

"Are you sure? I have to be out most of the day."

"I want to do some painting," I said, staring out the window. The sky over the park was a sure blue. Strong, white clouds rippled across it like bulky dinosaur bones. The colors stirred something inside me.

"That's a good idea, Aurora. Maybe it will cheer you up."

"Maybe," I said, not really listening but already

137

feeling the tingly desire pulse in my fingertips. It had been so long since I'd felt that.

When Nana left, I arranged the paint set, a cup of water, and a clean sheet of paper I'd torn from my new sketchbook carefully on the kitchen table. I slid the thin wooden paintbrush from its leathery loop in the case. Dad and I agreed that the brushes that came in paint sets were never very good; the bristles were always too soft. We liked them wiry and firm.

I drew the silky hairs across the palm of my hand. The brush was too soft, but it would have to do.

The colors in the box looked so perfect, neat and bright in their wooden beds, like tiny cradles, and I almost didn't want to disturb them. But my hand was buzzing so I dipped the brush in the water and then swirled the wet bristles around the cherry red oval. A familiar paint smell lifted up and got into my nose. It made my chest squeeze.

I let the brush hover over the paper for a minute before I realized that I hadn't even thought about what I was going to paint. *It's good to have a plan.*

Dad's voice sounded softly in my head. I listened for the rest, but nothing came. I swept the brush over the red paint again and waited. Still nothing. I could swear he had said more than that.

I touched the brush down and immediately red fingers of paint spread in all directions, making a shapeless blob in the center of the page. I tried to nudge it into a circle, but the more I moved the brush, the more the paint crawled in different directions. Maybe with less water and more paint it would be easier to control.

I cleaned the brush, partly dried it on a paper towel, and swept it over the green egg. Slowly, I let the tip of the brush graze the paper, and before I could stop them, muddy arms sprawled across the page.

My hand started trembling. Why wasn't it working?

I held the brush in the center for a minute, and it soaked a fat brown splotch straight through to the table. My hand was shaking and sending a shiver through my body. "What kind of plan? I don't remember!" I threw the brush at the floor.

Paint splattered the tiles, and I fell to the ground and started rubbing at them with a paper towel. "What's wrong with me? It's just a stupid painting. Who cares if I can't do it anymore." But a wail escaped my lips. Because if I couldn't paint, then who was I?

Finally, I picked myself up, found my knapsack in the den, and pulled out one of Dad's letters. Mom had given me fifty dollars. A taxi to Brooklyn couldn't be more than that.

Slipping past the doorman and gliding down Central Park West to hail a taxi was easier than I thought. And the ride to Brooklyn took only thirty minutes. Why hadn't I thought of this before?

There were three buzzers inside the building. My heart was in my mouth, but I found Marcus's last name, Hecker, and pressed #3 without hesitating. It took a long time before someone answered.

"Hello."

Even through the scratchy intercom, the voice was unmistakable.

"It's me," I managed.

There was a brief silence.

"Rory?"

The buzzer went off immediately and let me in.

Dad was standing in the doorway at the top of the stairs.

"Hi." His voice was thin and curled up at the end. He was wearing a faded gray sweatshirt, splattered with paint, and his hair was pulled into a messy ponytail.

"Hi."

"What — what a surprise." He hugged me and kissed my hair. My face was crushed up against his chest and my arms locked inside his embrace. I breathed the sweet paint smell of his sweatshirt. A clump of tears climbed into my throat and sat there.

"You look good," he said.

"Thanks." I shoved my hands deep in my pockets

and stayed in the doorway. I could tell that he didn't know what to say.

"Does your mother know you're here?"

"She's in Puerto Rico."

"Really?" His voice was a mix of surprise and anger. "Who's looking after you?"

"Nana."

"Does she know where you are?"

"She's out at some fund-raiser. She thinks I'm at the apartment."

"What if something happened to you?"

I shrugged.

Dad frowned. "Ror, it's great to see you, but what are you thinking? You can't just roam around New York City by yourself."

Maybe I shouldn't have come.

He finally shut the door and put an awkward arm around me. "Well, come on, now that you're here." He squeezed my shoulder and led me inside. Long, dusty shafts of sunlight fell through the windows into the airy room.

"Marcus is in Berlin for a while, so I'm looking after things." He spread his arms as if to embrace the space. "I know it's not much . . ."

I looked around. In the corner of the room there was one short counter with two burners on it, plugged into the wall. A refrigerator that looked like it had been chopped in half sat on the floor beside a milk crate filled with cereal boxes and bags of pasta. A small wooden table was wedged into the corner, with two mismatched chairs tucked on either side.

"You want some tea?" There was a rusty kettle on the stove, and he was filling it with water.

Across the room there was a double bed, a makeshift night table, and a folding chair with some clothes piled on top. Under the bed I could see suitcases, like drawers, stuffed with junk. A silver-necked lamp stood on the table, and someone had fashioned a shade for it out of a wire hanger covered with painted canvas. I didn't see any women's shoes or clothes lying around, nothing that looked like it might belong to her.

A roach scurried across the counter. Dad grabbed a magazine and clapped it. "These guys think they're my roommates." A limp smile crept across his face.

In a few minutes, the kettle started to hiss and he poured hot water over two peppermint tea bags.

"Is she out?" I asked.

Dad tried to sip his tea and burned his lips. "Who?"

"Your girlfriend."

"What are you talking about?"

Suddenly my tongue felt thick in my mouth, and clumsy. "You know I saw."

Dad's lips parted as if to say something. "It's not what you think . . ." he started, but then got quiet again. "I don't know what to say. I'm not sure you'd understand." His voice was funny, low and scraped-up sounding.

"You were kissing her."

"We got a little carried away. It didn't mean anything."

"So you don't love her."

Dad's chin pinched. "I haven't even talked to her since that day."

"Are you coming back, then?"

"I can't answer that. Not now, not yet."

Inside my head it felt muddy, like a bucket of dirty paintbrush water. "I could help out more with stuff around the house. I'll cook and do the laundry," I said softly. "I won't interrupt when you're painting."

"It's not that, honey. It's a lot of things put together."

Dad was just a few feet away, but it felt like there were miles and miles of space pushing between us.

"It's complicated, Rory."

"Like how?"

"I'm not sure I understand it all myself." He shook his head. "C'mon. Let's not talk about it. I haven't seen you in so long. I don't want to ruin this." He pointed with his chin to the opposite wall. "There's the painting I've been writing to you about." *145*

I turned toward the large canvas, resting on a narrow ledge a few inches above the floor. Small angular houses huddled together on a steep hillside, lit in beautiful bright greens and reds and browns, deep, true colors that he didn't normally use. A river flowed out toward the foreground, rippling in waves of gorgeous blue. I got up and moved closer. The whole painting seemed to glow. It was better than anything he had ever done before.

How could that be when I couldn't even paint anymore?

"What are you thinking?" he asked.

It was black inside my head. Nothing was making any sense.

"I'm not sure it's done yet," he said. "I have to look at it for a few more days."

I nodded and stared at the canvas. A sickness in my stomach was moving up into my chest.

"What are you working on?" he asked.

"I don't paint anymore."

He laughed. "What are you talking about?"

I turned to face him. "I don't know the plan. I can't remember what I'm supposed to do!"

The space between Dad's eyes got tight. "Rory, what are you talking about, sweetheart?"

"You could have called," I said. "You didn't even say good-bye."

Dad's mouth fell open, but no sound came out.

"Maybe Mom was right. We are better off without you."

His thin frame buckled from the words I hurled, like fists.

I grabbed my knapsack and started toward the door.

"Where are you going?"

"You don't care."

"Rory, wait —"

"I hope I never see you again!" My words pushed him back. And I flew down the stairs before he could stop me.

The sun glared a metallic yellow and sparks of

147

shiny asphalt glinted off the sidewalk, throwing stars in my eyes. Swarms of people were coming at me and cars reeled down the busy avenue. A siren wailed as I darted down a sidestreet and then another and another. Shapes and colors melted into big splotches, so I didn't see the man leaning into a phone booth until I knocked straight into him. He wheeled around. "Yo! You little twit. Watch yourself!" My heart pounded in my ears. A dog barked and strained at its leash, and I screamed even as I dodged it. Fingers of fear tightened around my throat.

Where was I going?

Then, before I even knew what I was doing, I threw out my hand to a taxi rounding the corner, and when it skidded to a stop, I fell inside.

the colors in my mind were too bright. They stung like sunscreen dripping into your eyes on a hot summer day. I wove through the crowds at Grand Central Station and slid my last bills under the glass partition. I didn't even hear myself say Hillview. I just grabbed the ticket and ran to my track.

The seat was cold. Outside the dirty window, colors clicked by in fast frames. Sailboats bucked on their moorings. I dug my fingernails into my arm until a little crescent moon of blood appeared. My skin burned, but it felt good almost. Making pain on the outside, where I could see it.

With my finger, I rubbed at the red smudge and then licked it away.

"It's complicated, Rory. . . ."

What did that mean? Loving people wasn't complicated. It was simple.

Inside, my feelings knocked about like bumper cars, spinning around in circles and hitting each other hard.

Before I knew it, the conductor was moving down the aisle collecting tickets, and the wheels were screeching on the track.

"Hillview, next stop!"

The doors slid open and suddenly I was standing on the platform in the sharp air. How did I even get here?

Cassidy was on top of me as soon as I pulled the key out of my knapsack and let myself in. I hugged him and let him lick my face. Then I threw my knapsack into the hall and flew back outside.

Cassidy barked and jumped and ran around in circles on the lawn before following me into the barn. I dragged a metal garbage can from the corner of the studio and started unloading stuff into it — drawers of pencils, erasers, and charcoal, paintbrushes, and unopened tubes of paint. In one swift motion, I batted an arm across a shelf of empty paint containers, sending them hurling across the room.

"What do we need all this stuff for anyway? No one is ever going to use it."

I tossed in scraps of paper, scissors, unstretched canvas, anything I could find that reminded me of him.

And then the phone rang, loud and shrill against the stillness. I let it go at least ten times before it finally stopped, and again, a few minutes later. I could almost feel him waiting for me to pick it up.

Now it was his turn to worry and hurt.

there were footsteps in the yard, crunching the cold, dead grass. Mrs. Morris, coming to feed Cassidy. I looked up as the door pushed open.

"Oh, thank God." Dad's face was hard and gray.

A stone sank inside my stomach.

"Do you have any idea how worried we were?"

I was sitting on the floor, rocking, and clutching Cassidy.

"Your grandmother called the police. She's a wreck."

"So what," I whispered.

Dad just stared at me. Without another word he went to the phone and started dialing. "She's all right," he said into the receiver. "You can let them go. Yes, uh-huh. I'll tell her."

He put the phone down. "You can't just disappear like that, Rory. I don't care how angry you are. There are other people you need to think about."

I just sat there holding Cassidy, who was letting out these low, pitiful cries.

"God knows what could have happened to you. Don't you ever disappear like that again. Do you hear me?"

"You disappeared first."

I could feel Dad's eyes on me even though I wouldn't look at him.

"It's irresponsible, Rory. You know that."

"You can't talk to me about responsibility."

Out of the corner of my eye I saw his paint-splattered sneakers scuffing at the wood floor. He kicked at a knobby board.

"I've never been so scared in my life," he said softly. "I could never forgive myself if anything happened to you." His feet moved closer, and then he folded up his legs and sat down next to me and hugged his knees. Cassidy's tail thumped against the floor as he nudged himself closer to Dad. "It was wrong of me to leave without explaining."

"Then why did you?" I still couldn't look at him directly.

"It had nothing to do with you, Ror. I promise you that." He gathered air. "There was this feeling inside me, like I couldn't breathe anymore. I don't know if that makes sense to you, but I thought it would just get worse if I stayed."

The wind blew and rattled the windowpanes. A bare maple branch gently tapped the glass.

"What about the mural? You promised."

"I think about that every day."

Dad pulled my hand from around Cassidy's neck and squeezed it. "I never meant to hurt you, Rory."

I remembered how he used to guide my hand over the paper during the drawing lessons, and for a few moments, I let myself be five again, until his voice pulled me back.

"I have something for you." He let go of my hand, and I watched him unzip his knapsack and fish out a small package. It was wrapped in handmade paper and tied in raffia. "I've been meaning to send it to you for the past few days."

For the first time, I looked at his face. It was soft and sad.

He put the package in my hands. "Open it."

I slid off the raffia and pulled back the tape very carefully so as not to tear the paper. When I unwrapped it, I stopped breathing. I just stared and then looked up at him.

"But how . . . ?"

He put his hand on my head and let it slide down my hair.

"It broke my heart to see you try to destroy it, Rory."

He took the wrapping paper from me so I could hold the sketchbook in my hands.

"I knew you needed to hurt me back. But all I could think was that I had made you want to hurt yourself, too."

I caressed the black cover, slightly warped but only a little charred. The spine was broken, but thick thread, sewn neat and tight, held it together. I opened it carefully. You could still see where some of the pages were burned away, but fresh clean paper was glued on from behind to make them whole again. I turned to the middle where the last drawing used to be. And there it was.

My tree.

He had repaired the edges of the page, but miraculously, most of the sketch was still intact. Only the tips of a few branches were missing.

"You'll have to finish those," he said, pointing.

I nodded, still taking it all in. My tree had survived.

"Thank you," I whispered.

When I looked up at him, there were small puddles of tears in his eyes.

"I'm sorry, Rory." He pulled me into his chest. "I'm so sorry."

Out the window, an amber sky flamed in the distance, bathing the river in color and light. I let his words and the familiar smell of him begin to melt away a layer of sadness.

"Sometimes I wonder why I keep painting," he sighed after a long silence.

"It's a process," I said, his own words coming back. "It's about watching and guessing and listening to the voice inside you. You taught me that."

Dad held me away from him a minute and smiled. "Picasso once said that every child is an artist. The problem is how to remain an artist once you grow up."

A blackbird tilted on its wing and landed on the maple branch.

"Maybe you can teach me," he said. "On weekends. This summer, if you want. We could paint together."

"Really?"

"Would you?"

I was nodding.

"I wasn't sure. You said you weren't painting anymore."

The sky blushed a deeper, warmer red.

"Maybe I could try again."

"I'll talk to Mom," he said as the last bits of light pulsed through the window and a golden feeling spread out inside me.

i found Mr. Miles hanging paintings in the cafeteria on the day of the exhibition.

"It's crooked," I said. "Go a little to the left."

He pulled a nail from his mouth and pounded it into the cork liner running along the wall before turning around.

"I thought you might need some help." I twisted the silver bracelet Mom had brought me from Puerto Rico around my wrist. Only three paintings were hung, and there were piles of canvases stacked on the cafeteria tables.

He lifted one and centered it on the wall. "That'd be great."

"Things didn't quite work out as we planned, the painting with my dad, I mean."

He pulled a tape measure from his back pocket and slid it along the wall to mark the next nail.

"That's too bad."

"A lot of things with my dad aren't really working out."

Mr. Miles finally stopped to look at me.

"He and my mom are splitting up."

"Rory, I'm sorry," he said and put down the tape measure and the hammer. "I had no idea."

I nodded. "I don't feel like talking about it now."

"Okay. But —"

"I know." I lifted a canvas off the top of the pile and handed it to him.

"It makes more sense," he said, taking the painting but not turning to hang it. "Why you've checked out from art. You've got to keep at it, though, Rory. You're too talented."

I gave him a real smile.

The next drawing on the pile was Dean's. I handed it to Mr. Miles and we laughed.

"Don't tell anyone," he said.

Before Christmas vacation, after all the pieces were handed in, Mr. Miles had brought Dean's drawing back to class and said, "If you want this shown, you're going to have to fix it." So now there was a big shield covering the warrior woman's breasts.

"You know, the nude is an important part of the history of art," I told Mr. Miles as he straightened the drawing on the wall.

"Try telling that to the school board."

I lifted another canvas off the pile while he put a nail in the wall. "Do they have the contest again next year?"

He stopped hammering. "Every year." He took the painting from me.

"Do photos count?"

Mr. Miles's eyebrows reached for each other *161*

above the crest of his glasses. "I didn't know you took pictures."

"I don't. But the painting I'm going to submit is too big to bring in. I'll have to photograph it."

Mr. Miles was nodding. "I think that might be all right. Assuming you let the judges come look at the real thing."

"Maybe you could come first, and tell me what you think."

"Just name the day, Rory, and I'm there."

colors swam inside my head. Beautiful dusk colors, so soft and yet so intense they burned away the hard edges of their forms. I was not thinking tree or river — I was thinking deep green, rich pink, and strong, steely blue. From these colors the forms took shape, one after the other, until the entire mural was painted across my mind.

The rattling of brushes and paint cans I gathered from the cabinet and set out on the table did not disturb the vision. I was fully inside the painting. Without hesitating, I dipped a thick brush in blue paint and pressed it right up to the wall.

I added different colors with the same brush, mixing the paint right on the wall. I liked the freshness of it, and the surprise, not knowing what would come. It was so different from Dad's method of mixing the colors on an old wooden board or in recycled yogurt containers to make sure they were right.

Like a skater who can form perfect figure eights on the ice without ever examining them from above, I was sure of every stroke. And I coasted through the painting like a seasoned skater, gliding along on shiny blades of paint.

It was much later when I finally stepped away. I stuck my brush in the bucket of water and inched back to the windowsill to see what I had done.

"Wow . . ." Nicky gazed up from the floor where she was lying with Cassidy. "It's amazing."

The colors seemed to sparkle, and even though the forms were abstracted, you could see exactly what it was. I tilted my head to one side to consider it.

"That's the great thing about painting," I heard him say. "You can create your own imaginary world to live in."

I thought of Mom then, coming home from Puerto Rico half a day early on account of missing me so much and not getting angry when I'd explained what happened with Dad. I remembered how Nicky didn't run away after I told her everything in one breath that I had been holding in for way too long, and her saying, "You'll always be my *best* friend." And that's when I realized you could also create something beautiful and real in the world you already lived in.

"Hey, you two!" Mom called from the backyard. "Could you come make the salad?"

Nicky kissed Cassidy's nose and stood up.

"I'll be right there," I told her.

"No you won't. You'll get lost like you always do. But I'll come get you."

I looked at my tree standing strong and tall on

the bank of the river, and it made me remember something. I slid off the windowsill, picked out a clean brush, and dipped it in fresh paint.

The great thing about painting is you can bring back something you've lost and keep it forever.

Carefully I arced the bristles around one more form, tucked beside a tree on the other side of the river, far in the distance, so maybe Mom wouldn't notice it when I finally let her come in here. But I would. It would be the first thing I'd look for.

Of course, it wasn't the same as having him here. But for now, it was something.

Maybe my father wasn't who I thought he was, or even wholly who I wanted him to be. Still, letting him love me in his own way had a good side, too, because it left room for surprises. I never could have guessed that he would rescue my sketchbook and work for all those months to repair it as best he could. But it was the words he wrote inside that were the most unexpected:

When you look back over all your old books, this one will always be the most important. It was the first one that was totally your own. You are an artist in your own right now. All you need, you already know. Just remember to watch the light and believe in yourself as much as I believe in you.

I looked out the window and studied the bare branches of the maple tree. Tiny green leaves already poked out. I could see the leaving time, all sides of it, and how everything that looks terribly bad can suddenly turn good when you least expect it. Like the sunrise breaks the darkness while we are sleeping.

I looked back at my mural, painted in bold greens and browns and blues and pinks across the barn wall. I saw my tree, standing strong and tall on the riverbank, its sturdy branches reaching for me again like outstretched arms. I saw this place, our world that was real, that I painted all on my own just for Mom. I saw my painting style, rooted in my father's but branching out in new directions that were entirely my own. I felt him watching from the other side of the river, and even though that wasn't where I wanted him to be, at least I knew he was there.

But most of all, in every solid layer of paint and within every sure stroke of the brush, I saw that I was there, breathing out the colors of my own voice.